FLEAGLE

the son of a ruddy duck

FLEAGLE
the son of a ruddy duck

by STAN HARDISON

introduction by MILTON CANIFF
creator of Steve Canyon

Donning

to my three girls ...

Shirley, Diane & Deborah

Library of Congress Cataloging in Publication Data

Hardison, Stan, 1933-
Fleagle, the son of a ruddy duck.
I. Title.
PN6728.F56H3 741.5'973 77-15075
ISBN 0-951442-45-0

Printed in the United States of America

CONTENTS

HARRISON

INTRODUCTION

This man, STAN HARDISON, is a Rebel!

He has defied all the ground rules for being a successful cartoonist! He was not born in the Middle West. He did not serve as an assistant to a well-known strip cartoonist who taught him the tricks.

Instead, he entered the field in the reverse order of the Bill Mauldins and other humorists who came out of the wars with big reputations which they carried into civilian life. Hardison did his soldiering, became a civilian commercial artist, then created the comic strip "FLEAGLE" which was later adopted by the Air Force Publication, TAC ATTACK.

FLEAGLE was dreamed up to help teach safety via the smile method, but, luckily, editors saw in this scion of a ruddy duck and a common loon a potential vehicle for humor which could reach the general public.

Like most of us, FLEAGLE, broken beak and all, has tried and fouled out too many times, but he continues to give life his best shot and hopes that some day the Great Fitness Report in the Sky will not Red Line him again.

Of course, STAN will not allow this to happen because it would crack the mirror held up to each of us in these incisive drawings.

Read on. It will be funny until up comes the one about you.

MILTON CANIFF

THE CITIZENS OF PEA ISLAND

FLEAGLE:

On a small island off the coast of North Carolina known as Pea Island, lives a bird named Fleagle. He is the elder son of a Ruddy Duck and Common Loon.

Unlike man, Fleagle was born with the ability to fly but this does not always work in his favor. Fleagle's life is full of large and small mishaps. He has a heart as large as his flight cap, enough nerve to try anything be it work or sports, and an ego that is forever being shot full of holes. He has that rare talent of doing almost everything wrong. For a bird with two left feet; or you could call him a square peg in a round hole, the citizens of Pea Island can't help but like him.

As goofed-up as Fleagle sounds, believe it or not, he is an ex-Air Force pilot. His many years spent with our boys in blue were also punctuated by the famous screw-up personality of Fleagle. By exemplifying what not to do when airborne, how to speak at the wrong time, and trying to get involved in everything has brought Fleagle an unblievable slice of notoriety.

MR. TALON:

Mr. Talon is the owner and operator of Talon Air Service on Pea Island. He is an old flyer who no longer flies and for reasons known only to him, he employs Fleagle. He is a stern boss with a gruff personality; but at times displays a dry sense of humor. Our only guess is that he keeps Fleagle in his employ as an example of how not to run an Air Service.

DORIS:

Doris is Mr. Talon's secretary and Fleagle's girl friend. She is smart and efficient in the office but a lousy cook. She is forever trying new dishes on Fleagle which most of the time means a few days in bed and a stomach pump.

At times, Doris gets just a bit tired of hearing Fleagle chatter endlessly about his many feats as a top-drawer flyer. Nevertheless, they keep dating so it must be love.

WALTER WIDGEON:

Like all ducks, Walter is an expert swimmer and with Pea Island's endless beach, it is only natural that he be the island's lifeguard.

Walter is the quiet type, liked by all because they realize his ability to run their beach. He is still trying to understand Fleagle.

MACAW:

Macaw is a South American Parrot who operates Pea Island's only cocktail lounge. Like all pubs or bars, Macaw's Lounge is the social center of the island.

Behind a bar and meeting most of Pea Island's citizens daily, Macaw is somewhat of a sounding post. He hears the good and bad and has the patience of a professional pan handler. He always has an answer which; most of the time, is deep and philosophic.

ROB & GRIFF:

Rob and Griff are a couple of bum pigeons who spend most of their day either fishing, playing chess, hanging around the airfield or Macaw's. Very few things upset them and other than Doris, they are Fleagle's closest friends.

Rob and Griff are the types all of us have met at one time or another. They just seem to move with the crowd but never get in the way; however, they are forever present when someone buys a round of drinks. How they exist is a Pea Island mystery.

FULMAR:

Fulmar is Fleagle's brother. He is a professional college student and can only be described as far out. No one can remember seeing his eyes because they are always covered with large mod sun shades.

Fulmer thinks all barbers should be replaced with rock guitar players.

He only comes to Pea Island when he needs bread. (That's cash in Fulmar talk.)

FLEAGLE'S MON & DAD:

Fleagle's dad is a retired clam digger. He has lived on Pea Island all his life. In some ways, he is very proud of Fleagle because of his tour with the Air Force. He is a strong believer in flag and country.

Fleagle's mom is the quiet, loving, and understanding lady that we all remember. She sees nothing but good in her two sons and husband.

VULGAR VULCH:

Vulgar is exactly what the name implies. His language is strong enough to dent a fender and he has the personality of a day old pizza. How he ever made it as a salesman, nobody knows.

FLEAGLE

I'M SUFFERING REAL BAD FROM INSOMNIA. I'VE TRIED EVERYTHING BUT NOTHING SEEMS TO MAKE ME SLEEP.
HARDISON
TRY TALKING TO YOURSELF.
© Stan Hardison, 1975
12-2

FLEAGLE

HARDISON
"BLESSED IS HE WHO CAN'T AFFORD VICE"
SEE YOU SUNDAY
HEAVY.
©; Stan Hardison, 1975
10-31

FLEAGLE

FOR THE LAST TIME DORIS, ARE YOU COMING ? WE'RE GOING TO BE LATE FOR THE CHRISTMAS PARTY !
HARDISON
I'VE BEEN TELLING YOU FOR THE LAST HOUR, THAT I WILL BE READY IN A MINUTE !
© Stan Hardison,1975
12-24

FLEAGLE

WHAT DO YOU BUY FOR THE SWEETEST, KINDEST AND MOST UNDERSTANDING PERSON IN THE WORLD ?
HARDISON
IN A CASE LIKE THIS, YOU THINK OF ALL THE THINGS YOU EVER WANTED TO BUY FOR THIS PERSON AND GO BUY THEM.
YEAH... MR. TALON WOULD LIKE THAT.
© Stan Hardison, 197
12-23

FLEAGLE

DORIS... IT HAS COME TO MY ATTENTION THAT YOU FIB OCCASIONALLY.
© Stan Hardison, 1975
DORIS
HARDISON
WELL, I THINK IT'S A GIRLS DUTY TO SPEAK WELL OF HER BOY FRIEND ONCE IN A WHILE.
DORIS
12-8

FLEAGLE

FLEAGLE, IF I'M GOING TO BE IN AMATEUR THEATRICALS, WHAT WILL PEOPLE SAY WHEN I WEAR TIGHTS ?
HARDISON
PROBABLY THAT I DATE YOU FOR YOUR MONEY.
HAR! HAR!
© Stan Hardison, 1975
A SENSE OF HUMOR SHE AIN'T GOT.
1-9

FLEAGLE

MACAW, WHAT'S THE DIFFERENCE BETWEEN A FARMER, A GARDENER AND A MIDDLEMAN?
PER PRESS
© Stan Hardison, 1976
A FARMER RAISES A LOT OF THINGS, A GARDENER RAISES A FEW THINGS BUT THE MIDDLEMAN RAISES EVERYTHING.
PER PRESS
HARDISON
1-15

FLEAGLE

MACAW, DO YOU KNOW WHY WOMEN WERE MADE BEAUTIFUL BUT DUMB ?
HARDISON
NO, WHY..?
© Stan Hardison, 1976
BEAUTIFUL SO MEN WOULD LOVE US, AND DUMB SO WE WOULD LOVE THEM.
1-10

FLEAGLE

ONLY CHEESE FOR DINNER...?
© Stan Hardison, 1976
HARDISON
YES... THE ROAST CAUGHT FIRE AND SPREAD TO THE PIE AND I HAD TO USE THE SOUP TO PUT IT OUT.
2-18

FLEAGLE

WHO SPILLED MUSTARD ON THIS WAFFLE, DORIS ?
HARDISON
?
BOO HOO!
© Stan Hardison, 1975
HOW WAS I TO KNOW IT WAS LEMON PIE ?
1-2

FLEAGLE

I'M SENDING IT TO MY SISTER IN ALABAMA.
© Stan Hardison,1975
SHE'LL LOVE IT. IT'S VERY RARE AND OVER 5 YEARS OLD.
HARDISON
YOU MEAN YOU PAID THIS KIND OF MONEY FOR A USED TREE !
11-5

FLEAGLE

FLEAGLE, WHEN WE STARTED DATING, YOU CALLED ME ANGEL. NOW YOU DON'T CALL ME ANYTHING ANYMORE.
YOU SHOULD BE GLAD THAT I POSSESS A LOT OF SELF-CONTROL.
© Stan Hardison 1975
WHY DO I SAY THINGS LIKE THAT...?
11-18

FLEAGLE

FLEAGLE, HOW DO YOU LIKE THE SALAD ?
HARDISON
IT'S GREAT. DID YOU BUY IT YOURSELF ?
WHAT DID I SAY ?
11-20

FLEAGLE
FLEAGLE, WHAT'S THIRTEEN LETTERS FOR OCTOPUS ?
HARDISON
AN EIGHT-SIDED CAT.
© Stan Hardison, 1976
2-17

Stan Hardison doesn't usually work under such close supervision as shown here. He works alone in his home studio in Hampton, Virginia almost completely isolated from the rest of the family. Stan does the daily Fleagle comic strip from the gag writing to the final inking, and most of the time delivers it to the printers.

Stan is also a full time art editor employed by the U.S. Air Force to head up the graphic section of the Tactical Air Command's safety magazine, TAC ATTACK. It was on the back cover of this publication in late 1969 that Fleagle found a home and grew to what he is today. A world famous pilot who can do nothing right.

When Stan is asked how he does the strip, his explanation is simple and his routine seldom changes. "I just walk into my studio, coffee in hand, sit down at the drawing board and start writing. I write about the first thing that comes to mind. If that doesn't pan out I change my whole train of thought and start over.

"Years ago I thought that the most successful way to keep a daily strip going was to

try and remember or make note of any gag or funny line I heard. I tried this for a while but it just didn't work for me. I soon found that the funny line I thought of in the morning would stay on my mind all day and by the time I got to the drawing board that night it had lost all its humor.

"I try to write at least a week of strips at one sitting. I don't think of expressions until I start inking because many times I find myself changing the dialogue at the last minute and this of course changes the expressions.

"I won't fool myself into believing that I turn out a winner every day. But I have found that the majority of my readers enjoy what I do."

So unlike Fleagle,
I must be doing something right.

FLEAGLE

I REALLY BELIEVE I WAS OUTSPOKEN AT OUR CLUB MEETING TODAY.
WHO COULD OUTSPEAK YOU? HAR! HAR! HAR!
HARDISON
© Stan Hardison, 1975
SHE'S GETTING STRONGER MACAW.
12-17

FLEAGLE

IT SAYS HERE, THE MAN WAS SHOT BY HIS WIFE AT CLOSE RANGE.
© Stan Hardison, 1975
PEA PRESS
HARDISON
THEN THERE MUST HAVE BEEN POWDER MARKS ON THE BODY.
YOU'RE RIGHT. THAT'S WHY SHE SHOT HIM.
PEA PRESS
1-8

FLEAGLE

MACAW, WHY DO YOU SAY PSYCHOLOGY IS LIKE A BELL ?
HARDISON
BECAUSE IT'S A WORD OF FOUR SYLLABLES THAT'S EASY TO RING IN TO DISTRACT ATTENTION WHEN THE EXPLAINING GETS ROUGH.
© Stan Hardison, 1976
1-17

FLEAGLE

I LOVE THESE LITTLE TEST IN THE PAPER EACH DAY. LIKE THIS ONE; CAN YOU NAME FIVE THINGS THAT CONTAIN MILK ?
HARDISON
YEAH. BUTTER, CHEESE ICE CREAM AND TWO COWS.
© Stan Hardison, 1976
2-13

FLEAGLE

HOW ABOUT THIS. A MAN EIGHTY YEARS OLD SWIMS A RIVER THREE TIMES BEFORE BREAKFAST EACH DAY.
© Stan Hardison, 1976
YOU LOOK LIKE YOU DOUBT THAT.
HARDISON
NO... I JUST WONDER WHY HE DIDN'T MAKE IT FOUR TIMES SO HE WOULD END UP ON THE SIDE WHERE HIS CLOTHES WERE.
2-14

FLEAGLE

FLEAGLE, THE BANK HAS RETURNED ONE OF YOUR CHECKS.
© Stan Hardison, 197?
HARDISON
THAT'S GREAT!
NOW, WHAT CAN I BUY WITH IT THIS TIME...?
1-7

FLEAGLE

WHAT ARE YOU DOING ?
TRYING TO ESTIMATE MY COST OF LIVING.
© Stan Hardison, 1975
TAKE ANY GIVEN INCOME AND ADD 30 PERCENT.
HARDISON
11-4

FLEAGLE

HERE IT IS OUR BICENTENNIAL YEAR AND I'LL BET YOU DON'T EVEN KNOW WHERE OUR DECLARATION OF INDEPENDENCE WAS SIGNED.
HARDISON
I DO SO...
© Stan Hardison, 1976
AT THE BOTTOM.
2-5

FLEAGLE

THIS IS THE SIXTH TIME I'VE CAUGHT YOU LOAFING THIS WEEK !! WHAT HAVE YOU TO SAY ?
TALON AIR SERVICE
HARDISON
I'M SURE GLAD IT'S SATURDAY.
© Stan Hardison, 1976
2-7

FLEAGLE

SIR, YOUR PAPER IS PRINTING LIES ABOUT ME AND I THINK YOU KNOW IT !!
HARDISON
© Stan Hardison, 1976
BUT SENATOR FLOCK, WHAT WOULD YOU DO IF WE PRINTED THE TRUTH ?
2-25

FLEAGLE

BUT SIR, JUST BECAUSE YOUR FATHER AND HIS FATHER WERE IN THE SAME PARTY DOESN'T MEAN THAT YOU HAVE TO BE. WHY, SUPPOSE THEY HAD BEEN HORSE THIEVES, WOULD THAT MAKE YOU ONE ?
HARDISON
© Stan Hardison, 1976

I SUPPOSE NOT SENATOR FLOCK, BECAUSE IN THAT CASE, I'D BE IN YOUR PARTY.
2-26

FLEAGLE

© Stan Hardison, 1976
I CAN TELL BY ALL REPORTS THAT OUR PARTY IS GOING TO SWEEP THE COUNTRY !!
TALON AIR SERVICE
HARDISON
IN THAT CASE FLEAGLE, WHY DON'T YOU START WITH THE WAREHOUSE ?
TALON AIR SERVICE
2-23

FLEAGLE
THIS YOUNG CANDIDATE YOU'RE IN FAVOR OF, WHAT HAS HE PROVEN THAT HE CAN DO ?
HARDISON
WHY... AH... NOTHING.
THAT SIMPLIFIES THINGS. AT LEAST WE WON'T HAVE TO BREAK HIM IN.
© Stan Hardison, 1976
2-27

A NOTE OF THANKS

Stan Hardison and Fleagle have earned a special vote of thanks from the 127,000 men and women of the United States Air Force's Tactical Air Command -- active and reserve. For more than eight years, Fleagle and his friends have given a distinct flavor to Tactical Air Command's safety magazine, TAC ATTACK, using wit, wisdom and humor constructively to impart a very serious message.

As an Ambassador of Safety, Fleagle promotes accident prevention and awareness not only within the United States Air Force, but in the civil aviation community and the air forces of other nations as well. We appreciate his efforts and hope he survives his predicaments to serve for many more years.

ROBERT J. DIXON,
General, USAF

☆ ☆ ☆ ☆

LEAGLE
YOU MAY OUT TURN THE F-4 BUT NOT ME !!
HARDISON
WRENCHED WISHBONE ?
NO ,TRIED TO TURN TOO TIGHT.
© Stan Hardison,1975

FLEAGLE
TREVINO, EAT YOUR HEART OUT.
NOCK!
230
HARDISON
BONK!
WHAM!
WHAM!
WHAM!
WHAM!
WHAM!
THAT'S THE FIRST TIME I EVER SAW AN EAGLE GET A BIRDIE.
© Stan Hardison, 1976

FLEAGLE
BUMP!
HARDISON
© Stan Hardison,1975
TOOLS
ZZZLAPSPITT!

FLEAGLE
LOOKS LIKE FLEAGLE HAS AN EMERGENCY OF SOME KIND.
SURE DOES.
HARDISON
BEAUTIFUL !!
MADE IT.
Ooo
TAXIWAY 1
FOLLOW ME
© Stan Hardison 1973

FLEAGLE
SURE WILL BE NICE TO GET HOME AND LOG SOME SACK TIME.
FLEAGLE, YOU HAVE A UFO EASTBOUND AT 10 O'CLOCK...FAST MOVING...ALTITUDE UNKNOWN.
UFO ? WHO ARE THEY KIDDING.
GREAT GOBS OF GNATGIZZARDS!!!
HARDISON
SPLAT!
SOME LUCK...I GET A CHANCE TO FLY ONE NIGHT OUT OF THE YEAR AND I RUN INTO A NUT LIKE THAT !!
© Stan Hardison,1975

FLEAGLE
NUMEROUS THUNDERCLOUDS, FLEAG.
HARDISON
SURE LOOKS BAD.
NEVER TRUST A WEATHER WEENIE.
ZAP!
THUNDERBUMPERS SURE FORM FAST IN APRIL.
YEAH, AND HERE'S AN APRIL FOOL THAT PROVES IT !
© Stan Hardison, 1976

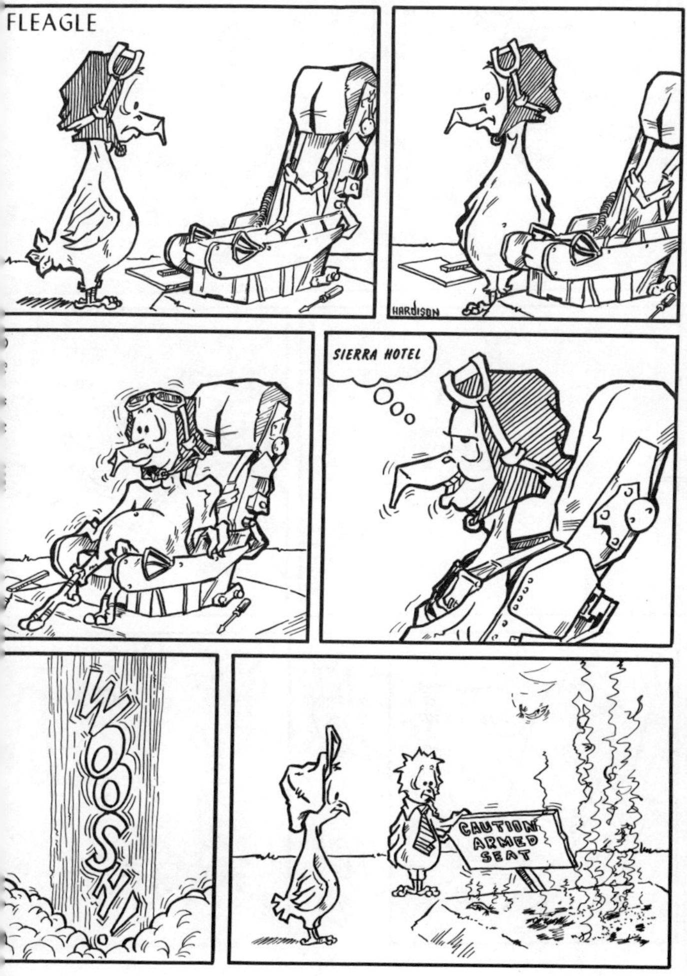
FLEAGLE
HARDISON
SIERRA HOTEL
WOOSH!
CAUTION
ARMED
SEAT

FLEAGLE
... MEANEST SON-OF-A-FINCH IN THE VALLEY ...
POP!
GOTTA GET OUT !!
WOOSH!
AN OSTRICH ?
NO, LATE EJECTION.
HARDISON
© Stan Hardison, 197

FLEAGLE
THE ICEMAN COMETH !
HARDISON
TAT-TAT-A-TAT
NO HITS
© Stan Hardison 1972
TAT-A-TAT
RAT-A-TAT-TAT-RA
RAT-A-TAT-
WELL, HE DID GET A FEW HITS.
YEAH... PRESSING.

FLEAGLE
SURF'S UP.
MAN !! LOOK AT THOSE TUBES !
HARDISON
NOW, WAIT FOR JUST THE RIGHT ONE.
WHEEEEEEEE
HANG 4
SURFERS MUST HAVE GOOD BALANCE, TIMING, SELF CONFIDENCE...
CRUNCH!
AND A LITTLE COMMON SENSE.
© Stan Hardison, 1976

LEAGLE
HARDISON
© Stan Hardison,1975
WHAM!
WHAM!
WHAM!

FLEAGLE
HARDISON
CHOP!
SNAG!
FFRUMP!
© Stan Hardison, 197

FLEAGLE
HARDISON
WOOSH!
© Stan Hardison, 1976
BLAM!
THIS IS THE WORST BICENTENNIAL I'VE EVER HAD.
?

FLEAGLE
WHY DON'T YOU LISTEN TO YOUR CONSCIENCE...
HARDISON
OR DON'T YOU WANT ADVICE FROM A STRANGER ?
ANOTHER BEER FLEAGLE ?
© Stan Hardison, 1975
11-8

FLEAGLE

THE WORLD IS ROUND. RIGHT, MACAW ?
WHY... AH, RIGHT.
PER PRESS
HARDISON
SO, IF I WANTED TO GO EAST, I COULD GET THERE BY GOING WEST. RIGHT ?
FLEAGLE, DID YOU EVER THINK OF BEING A TAXICAB DRIVER ?
PER PRESS
© Stan Hardison, 1976
2-4

FLEAGLE

MR. TALON, WHAT'S THE BEST WAY TO FIND OUT WHAT DORIS THINKS OF ME ?
© Stan Hardison, 1975
HARDISON
MARRY HER.
11- 21

FLEAGLE

THERE'S ONE THING I WANT TO MAKE PERFECTLY CLEAR!
WHAT?
HARDISON
THE FLOOR?
YOU'RE HEP.
© Stan Hardison, 1975
11-6

FLEAGLE

WHAT'S THIS?
A RABBITS FOOT. YOU CARRY IT IN YOUR POCKET FOR LUCK.
TALON
AIR SERVICE
THIS IS GREAT!
HEY..., BIRDS DON'T HAVE POCKETS.
12-11
© Stan Hardison, 1975

FLEAGLE

MR. TALON, WAIT A MINUTE... OOPS!
HARDISON
PLOP!!
I WANTED TO SHOW YOU THE GOOD LUCK CHARM I GOT YESTERDAY.
© Stan Hardison, 1975
12-12

FLEAGLE

I DON'T CARE WHAT YOU SAY. I STILL SAY A RABBITS FOOT BRINGS GOOD LUCK!
I HATE RABBITS.
© Stan Hardison,1975
12-13

FLEAGLE

FLEAGLE, THERE WILL ONLY BE A HALF-DAY OF WORK THIS MORNING.
HEY! THAT'S GREAT.
HARDISON

THE OTHER HALF WILL BE THIS AFTERNOON.
I MAY KILL HIM.
© Stan Hardison, 1976
2-12

FLEAGLE

I WONDER WHAT WOULD HAPPEN IF YOU AND I EVER AGREED ON ANYTHING!!
© Stan Hardison, 1975
HARDISON

I'D BE WRONG.
12-9

FLEAGLE
THERE ARE TWO WORDS I WISH YOU WOULD NOT USE IN YOUR REPORTS, FLEAGLE.
© Stan Hardison, 1976
HARDISON
SURE, WHAT ARE THE WORDS ?
ONE IS SWELL AND THE OTHER IS LOUSY.
1-30

FLEAGLE

COME ON DAD, GO TO THE GAME WITH US. YOU'LL SEE MORE EXCITEMENT FOR TWO DOLLARS THAN YOU EVER SAW.
HARDISON
DON'T BET ON IT BOY. TWO DOLLARS WAS ALL I PAID FOR A MARRIAGE LICENSE.
© Stan Hardison, 1975
11-14

FLEAGLE

I'VE BEEN THINKING DAD, MAYBE SOCIALISM IS NOT SO BAD.
HARDISON
© Stan Hardison, 1975
THE ONLY THING WRONG IS, WHEN PEOPLE LEAN ON EACH OTHER...
THEY SOON GET TOO WEAK TO STAND ALONE.
11-3

THE FLEAGLE T-SHIRT

Fleagle has had many bad months in his many years as a pilot. He has been blown up, beat up and burned up but he never fails to snap back.

But, along with the bad he has had a few good moments. One is shown on the next page, when Miss Stephanie Dowdy, Miss Virginia, 1974, made a Fleagle T-Shirt part of her wardrobe.

One of the highlights in Fleagle's life.

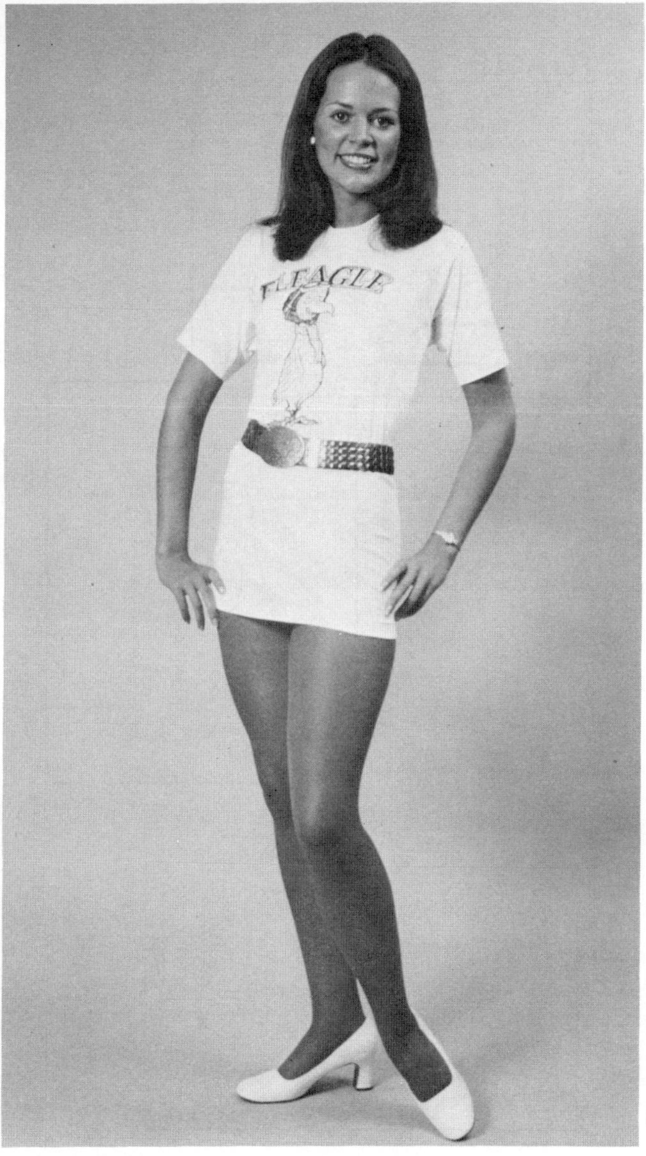

Photo by Joe Lahouchuc

Stephanie Dowdy, Miss Virginia, 1974

FLEAGLE

AND NOW LADIES AND GENTLEMEN, A SPEECH BY SENATOR FLOCK.
© Stan Hardison
HARDISON
CLICK!
THANK YOU.

FLEAGLE
NOW LET ME GET THIS STRAIGHT. AFTER YOU TURNED YOUR TV OFF, IT SPOKE TO YOU ?
YEAH !!
HARDISON
THEY DON'T BELIEVE ME...
© Stan Hardison, 1976
I DO.
1-20

FLEAGLE

I CAN UNDERSTAND WHY THEY DON'T BELIEVE MY TV TALKS TO ME...
HARDISON
AFTER ALL, IT IS IMPOSSIBLE.
HAVE A HARD DAY?
© Stan Hardison, 1976
1-21

FLEAGLE

NOTHING LIKE A HOT TV DINNER... MASHED POTATOES, TEA, OOPS, NEED THE SALT.
HARDISON
WHAT..!! WHERE'S MY DINNER?
BURP!
© Stan Hardison, 1976
1-22

FLEAGLE

WHAT'S THIS BALONEY ABOUT FLEAGLE'S TV ?
ICC
PEA PRESS
HARDISON
HE CLAIMS HIS TV TALKS TO HIM JUST LIKE IT WAS ALIVE.
YEAH !
ICC
PEA PRESS
THE FOOLS.
© Stan Hardison, 1976
1-23

FLEAGLE

FLEAGLE... ARE YOU HERE ?
HARDISON
HE AIN'T HOME YET. GRAB YOURSELF A BEER AND HAVE A SEAT.
© Stan Hardison, 1976
THANKS MAN.
ACCEPTED AT LAST.
1-24

FLEAGLE

GRIFF, IF A BOY IS A LAD WHO HAS A STEP FATHER, WHAT IS HE ?
HARDISON

A STEP- LADDER..?
HEY! THAT AIN'T BAD.
© Stan Hardison, 1976
1-13

FLEAGLE

ACCORDING TO THIS GRIFF, A MAN WHO GIVES IN WHEN HE IS WRONG IS WISE, BUT HE WHO GIVES IN WHEN HE IS RIGHT...
HARDISON

IS MARRIED.
THAT'S MEAN, GRIFF.
© Stan Hardison.1975
1-3

FLEAGLE

I'VE BEEN THINKING GRIFF, WITH THE ADVANCE OF WOMAN'S LIB, I WONDER IF THE TIME IS FAR AWAY...
HARDISON
WHEN A GUY CAN'T WALK DOWN THE BEACH WITHOUT BEING WHISTLED AT ?
© Stan Hardison, 1975
10-29

FLEAGLE
ROB, WHAT WAS GEORGE WASHINGTON NOTED FOR ?
HIS MEMORY.
HARDISON
WHY DO YOU SAY THAT...?
WELL, WE ERECTED A MONUMENT TO IT.
©. Stan Hardison, 1976
2-16

FLEAGLE

ROB, I DON'T UNDERSTAND WHY A GUY SHOULD NOT BE ALLOWED TO HAVE MORE THAN ONE WIFE.
© Stan Hardison,1976

I GUESS AFTER YOU MARRY ONE, YOU REALIZE THE LAW PROTECTS THOSE WHO CANNOT PROTECT THEMSELVES.
OH...
HARDISON
11-22

FLEAGLE

FLEAGLE SAID DORIS WAS REALLY SUFFERING LAST NIGHT.
WHAT'S WRONG ?
HARDISON
SHE HAS A SORE THROAT AND CAN'T TALK ABOUT IT.
THAT'S MEAN GRIFF.
© Stan Hardison, 1975
12-20

Fleagle could not resist playing his part in th
drawings ever done of old broken beak.

ale model fad. This is one of the most popular

FLEAGLE

MR. TALON TOLD FLEAGLE, " IF YOU'RE GOING TO BE ACCIDENT-PRONE...
HARDISON
TRY BUMPING INTO REALITY".
THAT'S CUTE.
© Stan Hardison, 1975
11-7

FLEAGLE
GRIFF, WHAT'S YOUR CHIEF WORRY ?
MONEY.
I DIDN'T KNOW YOU HAD ANY.
HARDISON
© Stan Hardison, 1975
I HAVEN'T
12-5

FLEAGLE

MR. TALON, WHY DO YOU SOMETIMES CALL FLEAGLE THEORY ?
© Stan Hardison, 1975
TALON AIR SERVICE
HARDISON
SIMPLE, HE SO SELDOM WORKS.
TALON AIR SERVICE
11-19

FLEAGLE

ROB, IN WHAT BATTLE DID GEN. WOLFE, WHEN HEARING OF VICTORY, SAY, "I DIE HAPPY"?
HISTORY
© Stan Hardison, 1976
HIS LAST.
THAT AIN'T THE RIGHT ANSWER BUT IT'S CUTE.
HISTORY
2-11
HARDISON

FLEAGLE

ROB, WHAT DO YOU THINK OF THE YOUNG CANDIDATE FLEAGLE'S BACKING ?
© Stan Hardison, 1976
HARDISON
WELL... KEEP HIM OUT OF OFFICE AND HE MAY TURN OUT TO BE A USEFUL CITIZEN.
THA'T MEAN ROB.
3-9

FLEAGLE

POLITICAL ECONOMY IS SURE MAKING THE NEWS THIS YEAR.
THE TROUBLE IS THAT IT IS OFTEN MORE POLITICAL THAN ECONOMY.
YOU'RE RIGHT ROB.

FLEAGLE
HEAR ABOUT FLEAGLE'S NEW HOBBY?
YEAH, ART.
HEY! WANT TO SEE WHAT I JUST FINISHED?
YEAH, FLEAGLE... SURE.
© Stan Hardison
5-5
Fleagle

FLEAGLE

FLEAGLE, I DON'T THINK IT WILL SELL.
WHY...?
© Stan Hardison, 1975
HARDISON
BECAUSE I GET THE IMPRESSION THAT IT'S OVER-PRICED.
5-7

FLEAGLE

FLEAGLE
MR. TALON, WHAT WOULD YOU DO IF YOU COULD TURN OUT A PAINTING SUCH AS THIS ?

HIDE.
© Stan Hardison, 1975
5-9
HARDISON

FLEAGLE'S ART TEACHER

FLEAGLE

HARDISON
FLEAGLE, I HAVE TO ADMIT, THIS IS PRETTY GOOD.
© Stan Hardison, 1975
10-18

FLEAGLE

WHAT'S ONE-HALF OF ONE-TENTH ?
TALON
AIR SERVICE
YOU DON'T KNOW!! ?
© Stan Hardison, 1976
WELL... I KNOW IT AIN'T MUCH.
TALON
AIR SERVICE
HARDISON
2-20

FLEAGLE

HEY BOSS, DO YOU KNOW WHERE WE FIND MANGOES ?
HARDISON
WHEREVER WOMAN GOES.
2-19
© Stan Hardison, 1976

FLEAGLE

HOW DID YOU ENJOY THE LIFEGUARD CONVENTION ?
HARDISON
GREAT, EXCEPT FOR THEIR BEACHES. NOW I'M NOT SAYING THEY'RE POLLUTED, BUT WHEN YOU PICKED UP A SHELL TO LISTEN TO THE SEA...
© Stan Hardison,1975
IT LEFT A RING AROUND YOUR EAR.
11-10

FLEAGLE

WHY DID FLEAGLE LEAVE SO FAST WHEN I CAME IN ?
PEA PRESS
HARDISON
OH, HE HAD A COUPLE OF BUCKS LEFT OVER THIS WEEK AND CAN'T REMEMBER WHO HE FORGOT TO PAY.
PEA PRESS
© Stan Hardison, 1975
11-15

THE HURT-HERKY

You don't call a trash-hauler a trash-hauler; that's a term they call themselves. You can call 'em tactical airlifters, C-130 pukes, hired killers, or just about anything else but please, not trash-haulers. Coming from outsiders (non trash-haulers) them's fighting words.

There are a few exceptions to this otherwise rigid policy. Presidents, monarchs, and other heads of state may use the term "trash-hauler." And Stan Hardison.

C-130 pukes have been known to commit an occasional indiscretion, like landing gear up or allowing an Army grunt to drive a tank through the tail of the airplane while trying to load it into the airplane.

Stan Hardison has captured each of these oversights with his hurt-Herky cartoons. And they have meant a lot to the guys who have flown the incredible C-130 Hercules. The cartoons have pointed out that even trash-haulers make a mistake every now and then, and through the cartoon medium Stan has branded those mistakes unalterably into the minds of every trash-hauler. Anyway you cut it that's accident prevention in its purest form.

That's why Stan can call us trash-haulers. Through his contributions to our well being and through the laughter he has given us while teaching us those accident-prevention lessons, he has become one of us.

Thanks Stan.

Tim Brady, Lt Colonel, USAF
former editor of TAC ATTACK

OUCH!!

Corns on my Goodrich

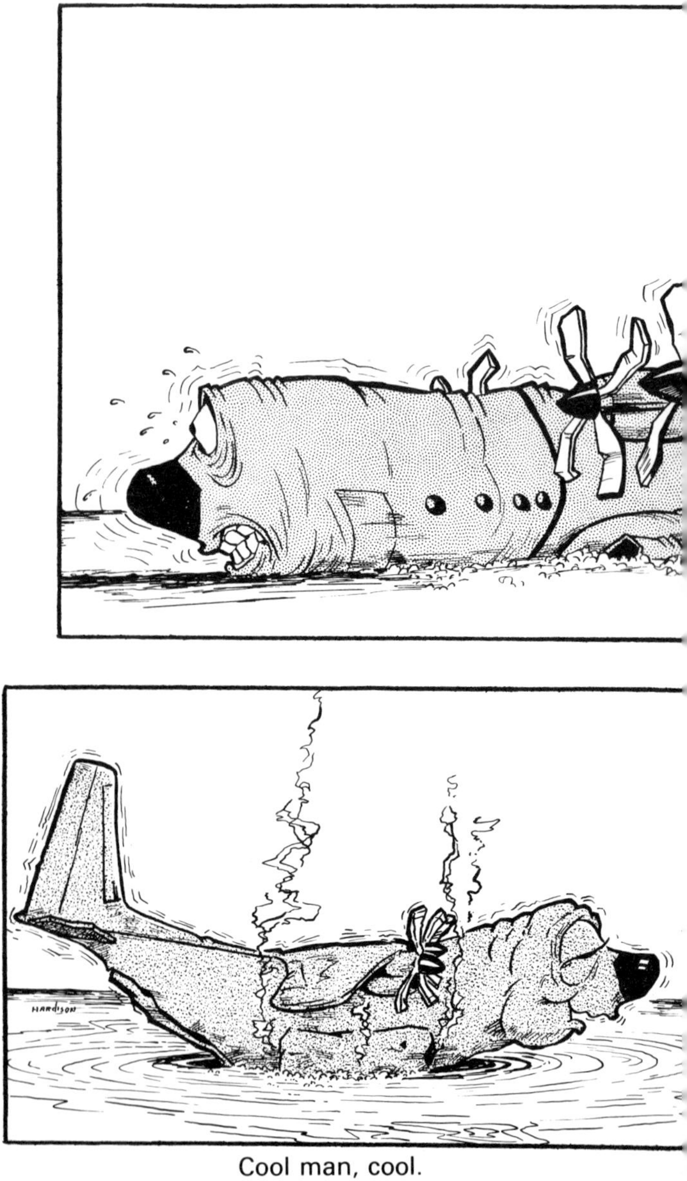

Cool man, cool.

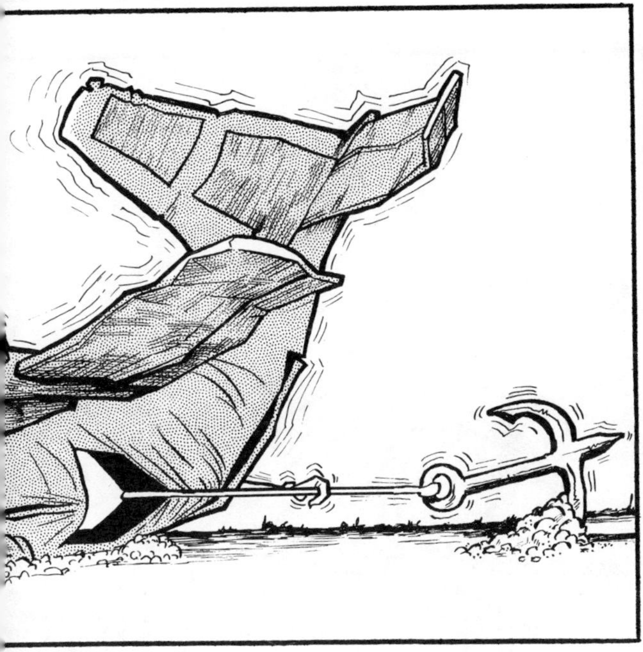

There has to be a better braking system.

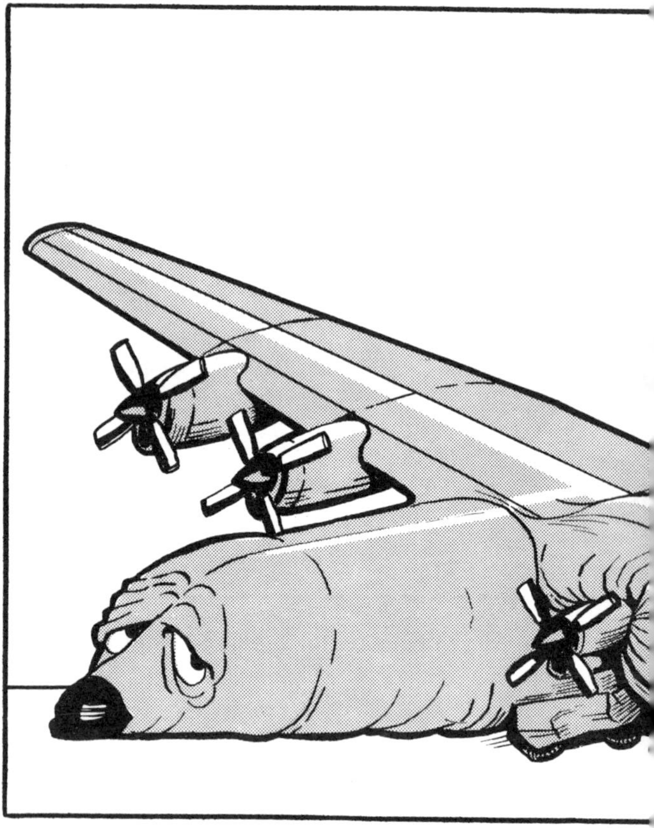

Just one mistake and I get all puffed up.

The back door!! you fool, the back door!!

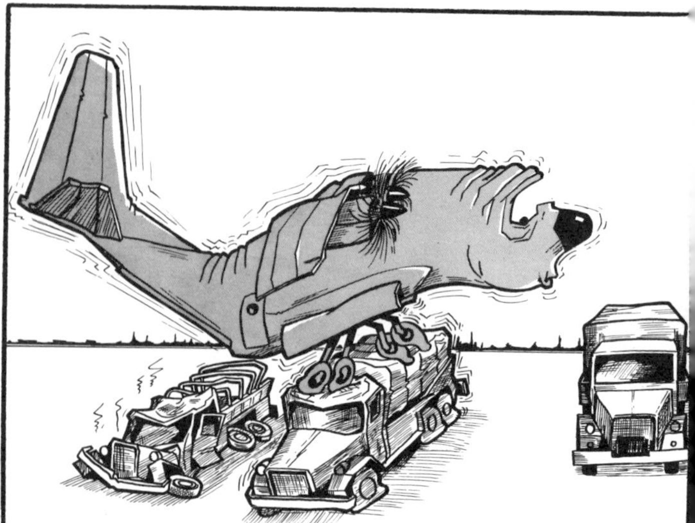

Tip toe thru the truck stop.

FLEAGLE

© Stan Hardison, 1976
YOU SHOULD BE ASHAMED FLEAGLE. WHY, WHEN GEORGE WASHINGTON WAS YOUR AGE HE WAS ALREADY A LEADER OF MEN!
TALON AIR SERVICE
AND WHEN HE WAS YOUR AGE, HE WAS PRESIDENT. HAR! HAR!
IT HURTS BUT IT WAS WORTH IT.
TALON AIR SERVICE
HARDISON
2-3

FLEAGLE

DORIS, WHY DID YOU CHOOSE LEMON AS THE COLOR FOR YOUR NEW YEARS PARTY DRESS ?
HARDISON
BECAUSE I HAD SUCH A HARD TIME SQUEEZING THE PRICE OUT OF FLEAGLE.
© Stan Hardison, 197-
12-30

FLEAGLE

GOING TO THE NEW YEARS PARTY AT MACAWS, MR. TALON ?
I GUESS SO.
© Stan Hardison.1975
1976
HARDISON
ON SECOND THOUGHT...
12-31

FLEAGLE

WHAT DAY IS IT, MACAW?
NEW YEARS DAY.
© Stan Hardison, 1975
NOW FOR THE BIG ONE...
WHAT YEAR IS IT..?
HAVE ANOTHER BLOODY MARY, FLEAGLE.
HARDISON
1-1

FLEAGLE

I READ THE OTHER DAY THAT IN SOME PARTS OF THE WORLD PEOPLE USE FISH FOR MONEY.
HARDISON

IT MUST REALLY GET SLOPPY IN THEIR GUM BALL MACHINES.
© Stan Hardison, 1975
12-6

FLEAGLE

BROTHER, WILL YOU LEND ME $20 BUT ONLY GIVE ME TEN OF IT NOW ?
WHY, AH.., SURE.
HARDISON
NOW, YOU OWE ME TEN AND I OWE YOU TEN. THAT MAKES US EVEN.
SOMETHING AIN'T RIGHT HERE.
TALON AIR SERVICE
© Stan Hardison, 1975
12-27

FLEAGLE

© Stan Hardison, 1976
I WONDER HOW LONG BEFORE I'LL BE IN THE POSITION TO DO AS I PLEASE ?
HARDISON
I DON'T KNOW FLEAGLE. NOBODY HAS EVER LIVED THAT LONG YET.
1-12

FLEAGLE

FULMAR, SOMEDAY I HOPE YOU WILL GRADUATE BUT THERE'S NOT ONE THING YOU HAVE LEARNED TO DO...?
BUT DAD, I DIDN'T GO TO COLLEGE TO GET A JOB. I WENT TO GET AN EDUCATION... DAD... DAD..?
SOB!
SNIFF!!
© Stan Hardison 1975
8-21
HARDISON

FLEAGLE

© Stan Hardison 1975
YOU TALK ABOUT IDEALS AND VALUES, BUT COLLEGE DIDN'T TEACH YOU ANY SKILLS. HOW CAN YOU APPRECIATE THOSE THINGS IF YOU DON'T HAVE ANY MONEY?
HARDISON
GOOD POINT MR. T. ...
MAYBE IF I WENT TO GRADUATE SCHOOL I COULD ANSWER THAT QUESTION.
8-23

FLEAGLE

PROFESSOR PECK IS A BRILLIANT BIRD. HE'S WRITTEN SOME BOOKS, CONDUCTED RESEARCH AND MAN, HE'S KNOWN ALL OVER THE WORLD.
HARDISON
IS HE A GOOD TEACHER ?
MAN, HE DON'T TEACH. HE'S MUCH TO IMPORTANT FOR THAT.
© Stan Hardison 1975
8-20

FLEAGLE

TELL ME FULMAR, WHAT'S ALL THIS TALK ABOUT ACADEMIC FREEDOM ?
HARDISON
© Stan Hardison 1975
LIKE MAN, THAT'S WHEN LIKE ANY PROFESSOR CAN TEACH AS BAD AS HE WISHES... DIG DAD ?
8-19

FLEAGLE

I LIKE CHEERFULNESS AND I ADMIRE ANYONE WHO SINGS WHILE HE WORKS.
© Stan Hardison, 1975
YOU MUST LOVE THE HECK OUT OF A MOSQUITO.
10-4
HARDISON

FLEAGLE
THAT'S A GOOD LOOKING PIPE. HAVE YOU TRIED IT YET ?
WELL... AH...
TALON AIR SERVICE
HERE, TRY SOME OF MINE.
I DON'T KNOW...
HARDISON
© Stan Hardison, 1975
THAT WAS MY FAVORITE BLEND...?
10-9

FLEAGLE

WHEN I WAS YOUNGER, I THOUGHT NOTHING OF A FIVE OR TEN MILE WALK.
© Stan Hardison, 1976
I DON'T BLAME YOU. I DON'T THINK MUCH OF IT MYSELF.
HARDISON
2-2

FLEAGLE

I HEARD A GOOD JOKE THE OTHER DAY. DID I TELL IT TO YOU ?
TALON AIR SERVICE
HARDISON
IS IT FUNNY ?
YEAH !
TALON AIR SERVICE
YOU HAVEN'T TOLD ME.
© Stan Hardison,1975
TALON AIR SERVICE
12-1

THE FLYING TIGERS

Fleagle pays a visit to a group of pilots from the famous Flying Tigers.

FLEAGLE

SEVEN COWS ARE WALKING SINGLE FILE.
WHICH COW CAN TURN AROUND AND SAY, "I SEE SIX PAIRS OF HORNS."
HARDISON
THE FIRST COW.
WRONG !! COWS CAN'T TALK. HAR HAR !!
I HATE COWS.
2-9

FLEAGLE

INFLUENCE: A THING YOU THINK YOU HAVE UNTIL YOU TRY TO USE IT.
HARDISON
© Stan Hardison, 1976
THERE'S GOT TO BE MORE TO IT THEN THAT...
1-14

FLEAGLE

OLD SAYINGS FROM WHO KNOWS WHERE:
" IGNORANCE IS WHEN YOU DON'T KNOW SOMETHING...
HARDISON
AND SOMEBODY FINDS IT OUT."
o o o o
THAT'S DEEP.
© Stan Hardison, 1976
2-6

FLEAGLE

OLD SAYINGS FROM WHO KNOWS WHERE:
"DIGNITY IS SOMETHING YOU THINK YOU POSSESS UNTIL THE BOSS SAYS...
HARDISON
WHAT IS THE MEANING OF THIS ?"
HOW TRUE.
© Stan Hardison, 1976
1-28

FLEAGLE

OLD SAYINGS FROM WHO KNOWS WHERE:
"A GOOD LISTENER IS A MAN TO WHOM IT IS POSSIBLE TO TELL A FUNNY STORY...
HARDISON

WITHOUT REMINDING HIM OF ONE OF HIS OWN."
oooo
I DON'T GET IT...
© Stan Hardison, 1976
1-29

FLEAGLE

OLD SAYINGS FROM WHO KNOWS WHERE:
" IT IS POSSIBLE FOR A MAN TO HAVE ONE WIFE TOO MANY...
HARDISON
AND STILL NOT BE A BIGAMIST."
OOOO
I DIDN'T KNOW THAT.
© Stan hardison, 1976
1-27

FLEAGLE

OLD SAYINGS FROM WHO KNOWS WHERE:
" THE SUREST WAY TO KEEP MILK FROM SOURING IS...
© Stan Hardison, 1976
HARDISON
LEAVE IT IN THE COW."
2-21

FLEAGLE

OLD SAYINGS FROM WHO KNOWS WHERE:
"IN POLITICS, IF YOU'RE AGAINST IT, IT'S A MACHINE; IF YOU'RE FOR IT...
HARDISON
IT'S A PARTY."
oooo I DIDN'T KNOW THAT.
© Stan Hardison, 1976
3-11

FLEAGLE

WHAT DO YOU THINK OF THE CANDIDATES THIS YEAR DORIS ?
© Stan Hardison,1975
HARDISON

WELL, JUDGING FROM WHAT I'VE READ ABOUT THEM, I'M GLAD ONLY ONE CAN BE ELECTED.
11-13

Photo by Joe Lahouchuc

Walda Patton, Miss Fleagle for 1976, she and Fleagle became very close.

FLEAGLE

I'LL MAKE A DEAL WITH YOU FLEAGLE. IF YOU WILL STOP TELLING LIES ABOUT MY CANDIDATE...
HARDISON
I'LL STOP TELLING THE TRUTH ABOUT YOURS.
IT'S A BARGAIN.
WAIT A MINUTE...
© Stan Hardison, 1976
3-6

FLEAGLE

DO YOU THINK AMERICANS WILL ALWAYS HAVE THE TWO-PARTY SYSTEM ?
PEA PRESS
HARDISON
YEAH... BECAUSE WE NEVER STAY MAD LONG ENOUGH TO GET A THIRD PARTY ORGANIZED.
PEA PRESS
3-10
© Stan Hardison, 1976

FLEAGLE

MACAW, DID YOU KNOW THAT ONE OF OUR LEADING NEWSPAPERS PRINTS ALL SPEECHES MADE BY CONGRESSMEN WITHOUT THE SLIGHTEST PROFIT ?
PEA PRESS
HARDISON
© Stan Hardison, 1976

YEAH..., AND THEY ARE READ THE SAME WAY.
PEA PRESS
2-24

FLEAGLE

MR. TALON, WHY DO PEOPLE KEEP WANTING A THIRD PARTY WHEN THEY DON'T KNOW WHAT TO DO WITH THE TWO WE HAVE NOW ?
DORIS
HARDISON
© Stan Hardison, 1976
DORIS, YOU'RE BEAUTIFUL.
GEE THANKS!
DORIS
3-12

FLEAGLE

BUT MACAW, WHAT WOULD BE SO BAD IF POLITICS HAD A THIRD PARTY ?
PEA PRESS
HARDISON
WELL FLEAGLE, IT WAS A THIRD PARTY THAT LOUSED THINGS UP IN THE GARDEN OF EDEN... THINK ABOUT IT.
PEA PRESS
© Stan Hardison, 1976
3-13

FLEAGLE

MACAW, SOME SAY IGNORANCE MAKES MOST PEOPLE GO INTO POLITICS.
WHAT KEEPS THEM FROM GETTING OUT?
HARDISON
SHAME.
© Stan Hardison, 1976
3-8

FLEAGLE

DID YOU KNOW THAT WHISKY HAS BEEN THE CAUSE OF MORE DEATHS THAN BULLETS ?
© Stan Hardison,1975
I DON'T CARE. I WOULD STILL RATHER BE FULL OF WHISKY THAN BULLETS.
HARDISON
11-25

FLEAGLE

MACAW, THE LAST TIME I WAS IN MEXICO, YOU COULD BUY TWO POUNDS OF SUGAR, A POUND OF COFFEE AND A JUG OF WHISKY FOR FOUR DOLLARS.
I'LL BET IT WAS ROTTEN WHISKY.
© Stan Hardison, 1975
11-26

FLEAGLE
FLEAGLE, HAVE YOU SEEN THE LATEST THING IN MEN'S CLOTHES ?
HARDISON
YEAH, WOMEN. HA HA HA !
LAST CALL FLEAGLE. FLEAGLE... ?
11-29
© Stan Hardison, 1975

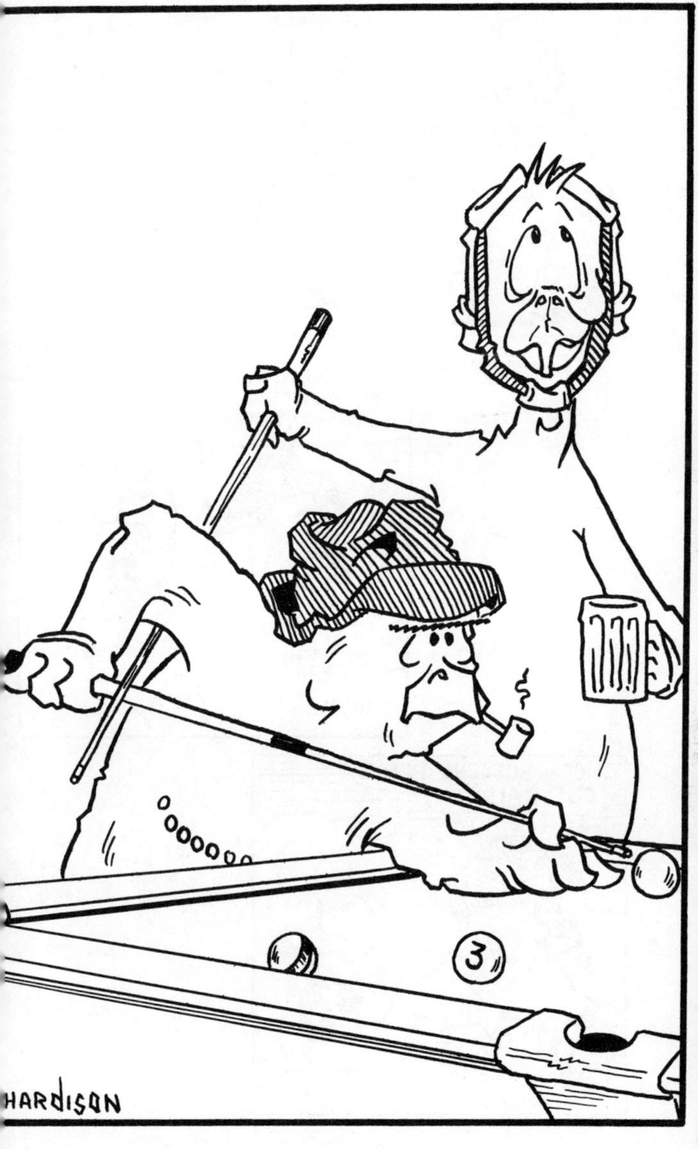
HARDISON

FLEAGLE

BET YOU NEVER SAW DANCING LIKE THAT IN YOUR DAY, MR. TALON.
HARDISON
ONCE- BUT THE PLACE GOT RAIDED.
© Stan Hardison,1975
10-13

FLEAGLE

MR. TALON, HOW DO YOU THINK GREAT WEALTH WOULD CHANGE YOU ?
FLIGHT LINE
HARDISON

WELL... I WOULD PROBABLY BE ECCENTRIC WHERE NOW I'M JUST IMPOLITE, AND DELIGHTFULLY WITTY INSTEAD OF JUST RUDE.
OH.
TALON AIR SERVICE
© Stan Hardison, 1975
10-14

FLEAGLE

© Stan Hardison, 1976
TELL YOUR BOSS THAT VULGAR VULCH IS HERE TO SEE HIM.
DORIS
HARDISON
VULGAR... THAT'S AN ODD NAME.
WHAT'S SO ▬▬ ▬▬ ▬▬▬ ▬▬ ODD ABOUT IT?
DORIS
11-1

FLEAGLE

THERE'S A VULGAR VULCH HERE TO SEE YOU.
HUH..?
© Stan Hardison, 1976
MY SECRETARY TELLS ME YOU'RE VULGAR !!
HARDISON
THAT'S WHAT MOST ████ ████ ████ ████ ████ PEOPLE CALL ME.
11-2

FLEAGLE

GIVE ME A ███ ██ BEER.
PEA PRESS
HARDISON
THAT'S NOT WHAT I WANTED !!
I KNOW... I LEFT OUT THE ███ ██.
© Stan Hardison, 1976
11-3

FLEAGLE

MR. TALON, HOW MUCH LONGER IS MR. VULCH GOING TO BE HERE ?
WHY ?
HARDISON
WELL... BECAUSE OF THE ROTTEN WAY HE TALKS, ALL MY POTTED PLANTS HAVE DIED.
© Stan Hardison, 1976
11-4

FLEAGLE

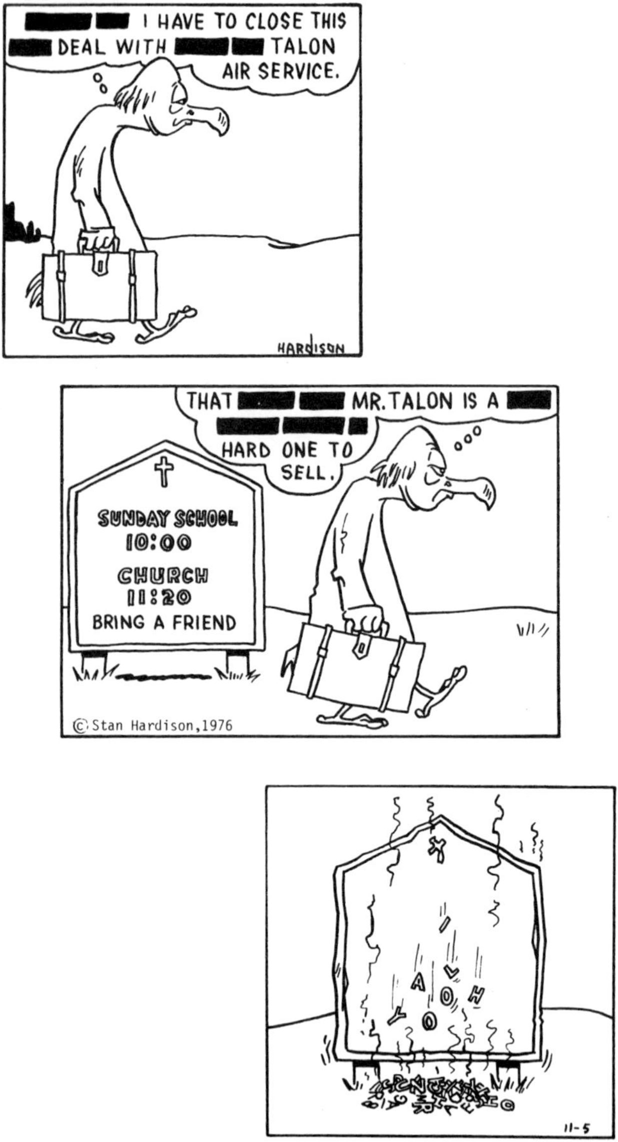
I HAVE TO CLOSE THIS DEAL WITH TALON AIR SERVICE.
HARDISON
THAT MR. TALON IS A HARD ONE TO SELL.
SUNDAY SCHOOL 10:00
CHURCH 11:20
BRING A FRIEND
© Stan Hardison, 1976
11-5

FLEAGLE
OH...?
YOU DON'T SAY.
© Stan Hardison, 1976
HARDISON
SORRY... BUT WE COULDN'T PRINT ONE WORD THAT VULGAR VULCH SAID TODAY.
11-6

Fleagle, trying to do his part at Christmas. But as usual, something went wrong.

A trick that only Fleagle could do.

FLEAGLE

I BELIEVE THERE'S AN OPENING FOR EVERYONE.
HARDISON
I'LL GO ALONG WITH THAT, FLEAGLE.
YOU WILL !!
YEAH... SINCE YOU STARTED TO WORK FOR ME I'VE BEEN IN THE HOLE.
© Stan Hardison, 1975
11-24

FLEAGLE

YOU KNOW, SO MANY OF US CAN FIGURE COST, BUT SO FEW CAN MEASURE VALUE.
TALON AIR SERVICE
HARDISON

IT'S GOING TO BE ONE OF THOSE DAYS.
© Stan Hardison, 1975
11-12

FLEAGLE

FLEAGLE, SOME MEN HAVE A THIRST FOR FAME, OTHERS FOR LOVE AND SOME, ONLY FOR MONEY. BUT DO YOU KNOW WHAT ALL HAVE A THIRST FOR?
HARDISON
SALTED PEANUTS ?
© Stan Hardison, 1975
12-3

FLEAGLE

DORIS HAS THE WORST MEMORY I EVER HEARD OF.
HARDISON
FORGETS EVERYTHING?
NO... REMEMBERS EVERYTHING.
© Stan Hardison, 1975
12-26

It just would not seem right to end this bo
What you see here is, to the best of my knowledg
he displays the Fleagle Family Tree.

ʲithout a small glimpse into Fleagle's past.
ıe only picture of Fleagle's den. This is where

REMARKS

"To FLEAGLE, losing isn't everything — it's the only thing."

→ MR TALON

"The average pilot, over a lifetime career, has .037 crashes. Unfortunately FLEAGLE never understood the decimal system."

→ WILBUR WRIGHT

"If I'd known that one day FLEAGLE would come along I would have stayed in the bicycle repair business."

→ ORVILLE WRIGHT

"I don't know if retired life will agree with FLEAGLE — he's always cheated at shuffle-board."

→ FLEAGLE'S MOTHER